The Adventures of
Mr. Seagull

Glenn Michael

Illustrated by
Jasmine Smith

To the shoreline communities of Connecticut

*Special thanks to the White Sand Beach Association,
the Town of Old Lyme, and all those who have supported
this project. Of course, a special thanks goes to
Mr. Seagull and his family!*

On the first day of summer, Callum woke up from his sleep early in the morning and quickly looked out the window.

Excited, he yelled aloud for the whole house to hear, "Look at that sunrise. It's SUMMER again at the beach!"

"Hi Mom," he said as he scurried through the kitchen and grabbed a piece of toast.

"Good morning, Callum—gosh, you are up early! I wish it was this easy to get you up for school!" Mom said as she smiled at her youngest child.

Callum laughed and pulled a golf hat off a hook on the porch and ran onto the early morning beach.

"Wow, there is no one even here yet. It's just me!" Callum said out loud.

"Whoa, not so fast young man. I am here, and so are many of my friends!"

"Well, who are you?" asked Callum.

"Me? I am Mr. Seagull, of course."

"Well, I didn't know seagulls could talk," an amused Callum inquired.

"Well I do, as you can tell; my friends and I talk all the time. In fact, I have been on this beach–and talking–long before you were born, young man," Mr. Seagull quickly replied.

"So, you live here at White Sand Beach, Mr. Seagull?"

"Why yes, during the fall, spring, and summer. But when it gets too cold, I fly down south to Florida."

"That is like my Nana and Pop-Pop–they fly to Florida in winter too. My mom and dad call them snowbirds. I guess you are a snowbird too!" Callum said with excitement and a big smile.

"Yes, south is that way, toward Long Island," he said as he pointed across the Long Island Sound. "And you see that gorgeous orange sun rising this morning? That is from the east where the sun comes up every day. Right over there between Orient Point, Long Island, and New London," remarked Mr. Seagull. "And at the end of the day, it sets in the west over by Griswold Point, the Connecticut River, and the Old Saybrook lighthouse."

"Can you see the Atlantic Ocean from where we are, Callum?" Callum nodded yes and was looking east at the sun rising over the entrance to Long Island Sound.

He then turned his head and looked west over toward Old Saybrook, where the sun would set hours from then.

"Wow, you sure are smart, Mr. Seagull. You know a lot about this beach."

As they walked along the shoreline and the small waves crashed onto the sandy, shell-filled beach, Mr. Seagull flew ahead of the barefooted Callum and pointed with his wing toward something.

"What is that?" Callum asked.

"That is litter, something that can ruin our beach! It makes me so angry. People take the beauty of this beach and Long Island Sound for granted," a disgruntled Mr. Seagull remarked.

"I will go and get it." Callum ran a few feet into the water and picked up some plastic wrap that was floating in the Sound as well as a soda bottle that had washed ashore.

He quickly ran up to a town garbage can and put the plastic and bottle into the recycling can. He remembered officers from the boating division of the Department of Environmental Protection in town had visited his school and spoken of the problems with pollution in the Sound.

Callum and Mr. Seagull spent the rest of the day together walking up and down the beach–all the way out to Griswold Point.

It was the afternoon now, and the beach had become crowded.

There were teenagers playing in the sand, families having snacks on the beach, and even some older folks reading under umbrellas in the shade.

Earlier in the day, Callum had run home and gotten a garbage bag, and he and Mr. Seagull used it to pick up any debris or garbage they found. Callum was proud of helping keep the beach clean.

As dinner time approached, Mr. Seagull and Callum came back to the family's beach cottage.

His mom leaned out and asked, "Where have you been all day on this first day of your summer vacation?"

Callum laughed and responded, "Keeping our beach clean!"

As Mr. Seagull was about to leave, Callum asked, "Hey Mr. Seagull, where do you and your family sleep?"

Mr. Seagull smiled brightly and said, "Oh Callum, that is a story for tomorrow. Go get some dinner, and some rest!"

About the Author

Glenn Michael is a writer, lawyer, and lifelong resident of the Long Island Sound. He currently resides with his family in Old Lyme, where he first fell in love with the Sound as a child. This is the first book in "The Adventures of Mr. Seagull" series, and he is available for talks, readings, book fairs, or interviews.

About the Illustrator

Jasmine "Jaszy" Smith is an illustrator based in Gulf Coast Mississippi. She graduated from MGCCC in 2017 with a degree in Fine Art focusing on illustration. She has been painting since before she could walk and is blessed to live her dream illustrating children's books and doing volunteer artwork for various animal shelters and charities.

Made in United States
Cleveland, OH
21 November 2024